Emotions Inked

By: Rotaract District Organisation, RID 3141

Lapsus Creations

Introduction

Rotaract is a global organization that aims to connect the youth and their ideas. This community holds networking powers throughout districts and countries. It is a worldwide organization of young men and women from the age group of 16-30 based in over 158 countries. Rotaract District 3141 comprises of over 90 clubs all over Mumbai and enjoys a total membership of 8000 Rotaractors. Rotaract District 3141 is one-step go for various vast and different fields and spheres of life. It encompasses varied areas like fun, community service, sports, writing, entrepreneurship and personality development along with a lot more. It works constantly towards giving back to the society and developing better leaders for the future. One of the many outstanding things about this organization is that it has a space for every individual and how it makes every member feel at home. It helps the current youth to find out what they're capable of while giving them a platform to showcase any talent they have or will to pursue at a large level. Rotaract District 3141 is constantly striving to achieve and excel while making more and more people from the youth a part of the Rotaract family. We thus pave the path for our members and those members in return, walk towards developing the society.

Emotions Inked is an initiative of Team Public Relations and Marketing of the year 20-21

Chairwoman:
Rtr. Sruchi Dadia

Officers:
Rtr. Akshaya Bandivdekar
Rtr. Manav Jain
Rtr. Jinal Mehta
Rtr. Vicky Gupta
Rtr. Muskaan Lakhyani
Rtr. Yash Thakkar

Acknowledgement

We wish to express a heartfelt gratitude for your valuable support

Rtn. Commander Jana: Rotary Club Of Deonar
Rtn. Girotra: Rotary Club Of Deonar
Rtn. Hema Subramaniam: Rotary Club Of Deonar
Rotaract Club of Bombay Filmcity
Rotary Club of Bombay Midtown
Rtn. Liladhar Parab: Rotary Club Of Deonar
Rtn. Major Priyanka: Rotary Club Of Mumbai Ghatkopar
Rtn. Parul Shah: Rotary Club Of Mumbai Ghatkopar
Mr. Pradeep Waghmare
Rtn. Radhika Pradhan: Rotary Club Of Mumbai Ghatkopar
Rtn. Ravishekar Krishnaswami: Rotary Club Of Deonar
Rtn. Rohan Dalmia: Rotary Club of Mumbai Downtown Sealand
Rtn Harjinderpal Singla: Rotary Club of Mumbai Ghatkopar
Rtn. Shankar Chawla: Rotary Club Of Deonar

Rotary Club Of Mulund

Regards,
Rotaract District Organisation.
RID 3141

Life It is!

Silence

In the echo of the chirp,
In the depth of the hearp.
In the vale of agony,
In the off beat symphony,
You will find me waiting to get acknowledged,
I'm the pause making relations damaged.
I'm solace, solitude;
The 'everything will fall in place attitude.'
Make peace not war,
This stands by my motto
To keep my destroyers afar.
Small talks favour me,
Heated conversations result in creating me.
You shall find me come up during a long drive,
Probably even on a romantic thrive.
I am satisfaction, I am misunderstanding,
I am love and I'm even an element of loathing.
Who am I? How am I all of these?
I'm the epitome of an introverts mind,
For,'Silence' I am;
Easy to figure and hard to make peace and find.

-Shivani Mokashi
ID: shivanimokashi410@gmail.com

A Selfless Love

A selfless love is rare to find,
It is the only one of its kind.
It is the one that always bind,
Not only hearts but also mind.
A mother's carrying her child in bosom,
Honey bee waiting for flowers to blossom,
Love which flows for all and not few some,
In all hard times, to rescue it will come.
Parched earth seeking cool rains,
Father toiling to take away child's pains,
Thinking without any loss or gains,
Loving with heart and not with brains.
Soothing shade given by the trees,
Deeds done without expecting 'please,'
Acts of kindness, done with such ease,
A smile that sure can, all hostilities cease.
Crops in the soil, looking for showers,
Words of warmth, that bloom like flowers,
It is the one with all healing powers,
In which love for others, by itself towers.

It is the one which thinks for the other,
And never for self, does it ever bother,
It is the one that only gives to another,
In thicks and thins, it stays together.
It is therefore, so very important for you,
To know whom you love and who loves you.
For, if there thrives a true selfless love in you,
That love will surely find its way back to you.

-Priyanka Doshi
ID: priyanka.matalia@gmail.com

Lesson of life

"Life is not good!" she said to him one day,
With his smile, he had very little to say.
The words that she then, heard from him,
Just shined so bright, in a light so dim!
Calmly he said, "Life isn't a bed of roses,
Especially with the challenges each day poses.
Life is never ever perfect for everyone,
But still it is lived, by each and everyone!"
She then thought about this and quietly
pondered,
How problems flew away, she really wondered.
Perhaps it's not the problem, but our attitude,
That drives away our joys, to the farthest altitude.
When one doesn't practise,
It's not right to preach,
But eventually this is what,
To everyone life will teach.

So let's change our attitude towards our life,
And strongly stand tall, against every strife!
Above was a lesson from a wise man to his wife,
Who taught her a simple way,
To live a happy life.
May God bless everyone
With abundant joys in life,
But the fact remains,
"No life without any strife!"

-Priyanka Doshi
ID: priyanka.matalia@gmail.com

The Expiry Date

A modern day fairy tale like no other
Started off with love and laughter.
A story of a princess and her prince
Without a "Happily ever after."
Their story began like any other-
A high tower, a locked up princess,
A young handsome prince, set out on his horse
To sought and rescue this damsel in distress.
She found in his arms, a whole new world-
A world she'd never known of before.
And in her eyes he found
Solace and love, they needed nothing more.
But every love story has an evil twist
And sadly theirs was no different.
For the world would never accept their love.
The Shakespearean play might give you a hint,
But unlike Romeo and Juliet
They knew beforehand of their fate.
For their love, although undying and pure
Already had an expiry date.

So as they parted ways, their love intact,
They chose to believe that they would be fine.
For the two broken hearts had in their time
together,
Found enough love to survive a life time.
So it's wrongly said that
A broken heart binds a man,
Never setting him free.
For, not many are lucky to ever find love
Even if it's nothing but momentary.

-Aayushi Kacheria
ID: aayushikacheria@gmail.com

When I Sleep

We are sitting on someone's terrace,
Talking about why
You like that particular song
And which line is your favorite.
Talking about how amazing it feels
When I start a new novel.
And between those talks
Touching fingers accidentally,
Little eye contact, and then light smile.
When I sleep I would like to go there
When you were mine and I was yours.

-Komal Verma
ID: vermakomal47470@gmail.com

Life Is An Ocean

Life is an ocean full of unknown faces,
Undiscovered, distant places.
Many of them that we've seen,
They were more blissful
Than anything has ever been.
Inspite of that fact every time
I think of that one face,
It feels like home, with him, in every space.
There was a tremble in the waves,
Merged into oblivion of essence,
And I spotted his presence.
He was like the roads of the town,
I never had the courage to go to.
His eyes deeper than sea,
More beautiful than anything could ever be.
Never knew the feeling I went out seeking for,
Was waiting right here at my door.
How would have I known,
As life is an ocean full of unknown faces,
Undiscovered distant places.

-Samriddhi Agrawal
ID: samriddhi2810@gmail.com

Life Is Not A Race

You are all over the place,
You won't breathe because you think it's a race.
You rush and push and hustle with time,
Wait a second, with your eyes so fine,
Look into mine.
Let the smooth breeze brush over your face,
Let your feet feel the waves
Whilst the sand of the ocean race.
Open your eyes,
For once let it be the starry sky you chase.
Breath, look into your soul and live again,
Look at the drops of the rain,
Smell the soil after the rainy stain.
Life is too short for us to care a lot.
Let the cool breeze brush over your face,
Because love, life is not a race.

-Samriddhi Agrawal
ID: samriddhi2810@gmail.com

Defeated War

I'm walking towards something,
A light I might be following,
Head not that high, unsure of what I'm feeling.
My frightened soul and the heavy breathing,
Lonely and no conscious healing.
I can sense my thoughts drowning,
Aware of it going down hill
With no change in gear.
It's getting darker on this path,
Racing questions in my mind,
Why am I here? Who put me here?
How long am I going to be here for?
I can hear faint noises, my feet getting colder,
There's this constant disappointment,
It just doesn't seem to disappear.
Suddenly, I'm being dragged further,
There's little to no visibility ahead,
Why can't I just keep my head straight
And command my body to follow?

Its like I'm being pushed, shoved to be precise,
It's pitch black and I'm petrified.
Gasping as the aura of disaster is taking over,
I'm losing my left over control,
You could hear my soul giving up,
On this little war of my own.
I was late and out of luck,
Lost my peace of mind,
There was no path left to follow,
After this defeated war of mine.

-Tehseen Zariwalla
ID: tzariwalla@gmail.com

The Journey Of Life

We enter the universe for a fleeting while,
Embracing humanity
Through our families with a smile.
The mischief of childhood,
Those games in the park,
Slowly graduate to a reality that is stark.
Education and employment
Becomes the need of the hour,
The rat race continues, in the struggle for power.
In the midst of this madness,
Our soul mates we find,
Changing the trajectory
Of our heart and our mind.
The footsteps of children adorn our days,
As we are drawn to their lives and their ways.
But soon autumn arrives, with aging and pain,
And we question ourselves was it all in vain?
Or was it a life that I would live anew.
The answer my friends is it all up to you.
Live in the moment, dance in the rain,
For this moment in time will never be yours
again.

-Celeste Pereira
ID: celeste0304pereira@gmail.com

Dead Asleep

Never did she laugh,
Never did she cry,
Never did she tell the truth,
Never did she lie,
She was alone and fell asleep.
Happy she was, wanted she was,
Laughed a lot, played a lot,
Everything was perfect,
When she realized it was just a dream.
She woke up expecting a new start,
It was actually a new start,
With a suffering end, in heaven.

-Adishri Gupta
ID: adishrigupta16@gmail.com

The Devil's Liar

She screamed in agony,
As the blood gushed out from her rash,
It flowed, and made her dizzy
From the gory sight.
She gazed around desperately for some aid,
While holding in another cry
As her teeth gnashed.
All she could perceive were the gnarly
And grimacing foliage
Bowing under the moonless night.
Stagnant murky waters and
The submerged bridge remained there,
Untouched, undisturbed and unpleasant
everything stood.
The pungent smell of some unearthly being
And decay filled the air.
Not even a hum of bird or the "Plop plop"
Popping of the bubbles
Oozing in the muds in these woods.
So intrigued, she was,
Couldn't handle the untamed curiosity
And the unexplainable pull towards this forest.
Crazy stories flooded in her village
And the horror-struck folks
Who had managed to come back.

She was different though,
Wouldn't sit and wonder
About the unknown and
Not explore like the rest.
Suddenly broken out of the reverie
By a series of whispers in the abyss so black,
Turning her head around
Rapidly to find the source,
Someone who could salvage her
From the pickle she had landed herself in,
All she was met was disappointment and the fear
That clawed her being and
A shudder that shook her body.
Alone alone all alone,
Alone in a situation she has never been,
Gleaming red eyes followed
With each step she took
And she regretted listening nobody.
Choosing a path she could've averted
Was a definite wise folly,
As creepy as it already was,
She couldn't shake a sinister aura following her.
Loopy Lucy, so loopy and dim she was,
To lose the vigilance of her surrounding.
Halted at the sight of an innocent being,
A cute and adorable girl of age around five.

Staring right at her
With those bottomless and empty eyes,
Head tilted and arms with a doll dangling,
Lucy fell right into it,
The trap schemed for the naive.
Lucy reached out to her,
Hoping to help the little one
In this ominous and menacing death front -
Burned and hurt,
Excruciating pain and betrayal was all she got.
The evil had found another victim to hunt,
It sucked her soul, leaving her gasping for life,
As she feebly fought.
It turned with a malicious smile evident, returning
to its lair,
Feeding on the innocent,
It now laid satisfied for the day,
Caressing it's sickly skin and grimacing hair,
As it waited timelessly for its next prey.

-Mahek Sota
ID: rtrmaheksota@gmail.com

Angel Of Theft

There once was a thief, his name was Smile.
The sweet charm of his, trailed a thousand mile.
Been a victim of him, over and over again.
Inevitably falling in love with his style.
But then one fine morning,
I heard he was gone...
With an angel flying, at the crack of dawn.
I keep now amassing, a treasure blue and gold.
Hopelessly hoping, he might steal it once more!!!

-ReyHan
ID: sshreyang@gmail.com

Time - They Say...

They say time is just another dimension,
That we can travel through.
But they never told us how two people can be,
In different times, at the same time!
They say time heals everything,
That it can make you forget all pain.
But they never told us,
How it only takes back the memories
And leaves the pain all the same!
They say time is money,
That you must treasure each moment.
But they never told us
How there are no banks to deposit time,
Or none that lets you borrow it.
They told me to let it go,
That past never lets you be in the present.

But I couldn't tell them
How no present can ever compare my past,
For no future can have you in it.
They don't talk about you now,
That your name might trigger the sadness.
But I cannot tell them
How every day since you're gone is shit,
That every thought without you is madness.

-ReyHan
ID: sshreyang@gmail.com

Dosvedanya - Until Next Time

A lump in the throat,
A hunch of impending homesickness,
A lesson or two learnt on hope,
A longing to let go disdain,
And a piece of soul; gained,
From this trade which started
And ended in the rains.

-Natalia Sunil Poojari
ID: natalia.sunil.poojari@gmail.com

The loop

Strange is this madness
That runs from itself a labyrinth of uncertainty.
The chase of contentment,
The constant tug of war.
Between illusion and reality;
Conscious, unconscious,
To wake only to sleep,
To sleep only to dream.
I have nothing to prove,
Yet, smeared with evidence.
I have no place to go.
Yet, always arriving.
In moving forward,
Something was left behind.
I'm always in hiding.
But want to be found.
What can you lose?
Everything but your mind.
And nothing escapes itself,
Eternity goes on, forever.
You think you're alone,

But you're always being followed.
Strange is this madness
Till it meets itself.

-Rukhsar Shaikh
ID: rukhsar.rs@gmail.com

The Beginning Of End

In the beginning you will feel a slight pain,
All the memories will rewind down the lane.
But don't you forget to call his name,
Because life is a game which no one can claim.
After all, everything ends the same.
You will feel a slight pain
But remember nothing will go in vain.

-Priyanka Patil
Email ID: priyankapatil216@gmail.com

Teenage- Life's First Quest

"We had it tough, you have plethora of options."
Have you heard this before,
A parent's age old diction?
Yes, we have options,
The choices are unlimited,
But we've had our share
Of problems, confusion, stress
And the need for being exquisite.
"Learn to play a sport,
A foreign language is a must,
Be good in studies,
Find a job that lasts."
Teenage to me is the toughest bit,
Of a live that remains well lit,
The childhood essence of innocence is lost,
And the right to give your opinion
Comes at a high cost.
Hence, dear parents, I humbly request,
Don't make school life your child's major quest,
It's natural for us to falter along,
Tumble and get back up
To nowhere we actually belong.

-Dhritti Shah
ID: shahdhritti@gmail.com

Boat Of Hope

"Who can hear your cries, tell me?
They are like sand-castles on a shore.
Screaming as loud as you can,
Washed away by waves, and are no more.
The waves are momentary,
But their sights set high.
Like of sparrows with little wings,
Who never reach the skies.
So you hold on, in this boat of hope,
Waiting for the thirst to end.
And in this dark storm,
Horizon will come,
If you make the sea, your friend."

-Rtr. Ishaan Patil
ID: Ishaanpatil96@gmail.com

Celebrating Lives

It is necessary to have controversy,
Life is exactly that;
A paradox and an oxymoron
At the drop of a hat.
Between the belligerent blacks
And the withering whites,
Life is the grey,
The flight of the highlights.
We aren't going anywhere,
There isn't any destination,
A simple gesture or some kind words,
It's that elation.
The sync between friends and foes,
The according balance,
The compassion is what counts,
Its seldom the distance.
The memories abode,
By the day, by the year,
Every step, every chore,
Each smile, each tear.
So many divine handsel
To sum up in a parody!

Isn't that enough reason to rejoice,
To jubilate already?
Come let's celebrate the life
That has been given,
A bestowal of love,
Of hope in our tiny bit of heaven.

-Nikhil Sabnani
ID: nikhil009sabnani@gmail.com

Once Upon A Time

Once upon a time - Quarrelled, ranted, whined,
Never imagined Mumbai
To be so quiet, serene and enchanting.
With the cars parked and the skies filled with
sparrows and lark;
The Bustling city, which never sleeps is at home,
Pondering deep with days to come
And happy to spend time with their closed ones;
The chatter and banter,
Slowing down no more
The aunties ferrying the markets,
With bags and in gowns.
The city that never sleeps,
Has slept well praying for recovery of those,
Where COVID-19 dwells,
It shall rise back, back on its feet.
Once we overcome the virus,
The city bit more clean and neat.
Yet, I guess we shall all ponder,
Do we really need to live back in that bustling
streets?
Do you?

- Trilok Prabhakaran
ID: trilok.pr@gmail.com

Keep Moving In This Movie Called Life

I know you have moved mountains
And there are still many more to be moved,
Not sure about all being filled
With happiness and joy,
Some might include a bit of dilemma or sadness,
Some might be confusing,
Some such you barely have any idea about,
Above this what stands is your will
To cross all of them no matter how they are;
Which maybe filled with joy, misery, terror or
Any other aspect in life.
I am no more the little girl who used to get
Scared, even if 20 bad eyes grope me.
All I want is nothing more,
It's just to see myself happy again,
It's not to belittle myself on the basis of all the
Odds the near and dear one's have done to me;
Maybe I should cry over things,
And I would surely cry
Only if I was willing to cry!
But I am willing to take chances and
To explore the way things go;
Not here to look for how someone else
Might behave and grin at me,

I am here to look for my well-being
Not knowing where this way goes!
Where does this road brings me up to,
I barely know anything about tomorrow,
But all I know is life is a journey
And nothing is permanent,
If not happiness then
Why not fuck sadness and it's pain/ache?

-Maitri Gada
ID: rtr.maitrigada@gmail.com

Here Comes Love!

Thinking About You

Days passed by thinking about you.
How I wish to hold you tonight
Beneath the Azure sky!
Feeling lost in time
Thinking if you're mine.
To make me feel more alive,
Until you arrive.

-Nidhi Shah
ID: nidhishah1920.ns@gmail.com

I Wish I Knew Her Name

We were in the bus,
Our eyes met when I sat in front of you.
I tried to look at you again and again
When you were trying to tie your hair up.
It was your third attempt
To get a perfect ponytail.
And with attempts your face was becoming
More annoying and attractive at the same time.
I felt something, I felt less tired.
I should have asked your name.

-Komal Verma
ID: vermakomal47470@gmail.com

You stay

Take a closer look,
And you'll realize how ugly,
Messed up,
Broke,
Lonely,
Tired they are.
And that's when
YOU STAY

-Komal Verma
ID: vermakomal47470@gmail.com

Keeper

It's all about not changing the song
Even it is not interesting anymore.
It's about not throwing the old jeans,
Even it's not wearable anymore.
It's about keeping that wine,
Even when it's not magical anymore.
Because, it's about finding a new beat
Every time you hear it,
Finding more comfort in that old jeans and
Feeling the magic in the fine wine.
It's about exploring and keeping
The oxytocin flowing in our veins,
Whether it is your favorite thing or a person.

-Coco
ID: cocotales47@gmail.com

Enlightened Smile

"KNOCK KNOCK,"
She knocked each glass pane,
Unknowingly, learning to thrive in hurricane.
On the signal stopped all the cars,
None gave humbly and
Had enough to spend in bars.
Saw her on street with 3 lights,
Asking a rupee or two for her daily bites.
Feeding family, large burden on small shoulders,
She was strong enough like Titanic builders.
Finally came by our window,
With habit of listening away GO,
But, in a hope to take home some dough.
Daddy danger peeped out like ducks,
And handed her 10 bucks.
With huge smile on face,
He greeted HAPPY DIWALI.
Her smile was like millions of lamp
In the city of BALI.

-Aryan Pawar
ID: aryan.a.pawar@gmail.com

Soul

The amazing soul that can
Clean your heart with truthfulness,
Disease it with lies,
Break it with just a drop of tear,
Mend it with a thread of love.
A conspicuous soul that
Can outshine your physical beauty,
The brightest sun covering the flaws,
The mountain of thoughts,
Makes you peculiar.
The hideous soul that
Connects your mind with the heart,
The sea of your emotions,
The root of your values,
The seed of your life.

-Nandana Mukherjee
ID: nandanamukherjee05@gmail.com

Dance With Me

On a clammy summer day,
While wandering on a populated beach,
My eyes caught (found) you!
You were deeply lost in a novel,
DANCE WITH ME it said.
My heart raced as I saw you.
So gentle, so calm, so fragile.
Yet, you sat there on that hot beach bench
Facing the cruel Sun.
I hate that Sun for tanning your beautiful skin,
I felt jealous of that sun,
For seeing you everyday.
As I approached you,
My heart tried to leap out,
Just then I saw a flicker of emotions
On your angelic face,
I wanted to erase that anguish,
But the cause was unknown to me.
A minute later,
Your tensed feature turn into a bright beam!!
I instantly thanked God!
I never ever want to see,
That dreadful expression on your face.
I bend down on knees asking, Dance with me?
You seemed doubtful.

What happened next was,
The most beautiful part of the day!
You were there in my arms,
Holding onto me tightly,
Gently rocking on the music.

-Bhavya Gupta
ID: bhavya13994@gmail.com

Writing You...

Your skin like an open canvas,
My feelings write the sweetest lyrics on it.
Our pouts do a passionate converse,
As the strongest intoxication hits.

While penning down my emotions you moan,
As you decipher the meaning of every word.
Like the moonlight
On the darkest path you shone,
Holding you close to me is always preferred.

I won't ever run out of pages,
As your body and soul for me are immortal.
For this want for peace I rove for ages,
As I am teleported to another portal.

For all the battles I fought,
You brought tranquility to me.
For all the sins I wrought,
You brought salvation to me.

-Aniket Naik
ID: aniket.naik@yahoo.in

That One Day

That one day came just once and stayed forever.
Little did I know, I'd see you never?
Those few hours brought a smile on my face,
Now you aren't there and I can find no trace.
I laughed, I danced, I expressed.
Until this day, I have no regrets.
No pictures, no pouts,
Even when you're gone,
I have no doubts.
That one day will always be mine,
Esteeming it my smile shall shine.
I may be embarrassing with those moves,
But thank you
For embracing them without any blues.
You may or may not come back, that's okay,
I will own those memoirs today and every day.
How I wish you weren't like
You said you weren't,
We parted ways like known strangers.
That one day was about me and my happiness,
You were there then and now there is no
sparseness.

-Gayatri Jhaveri
ID: gayatrijhaveri@gmail.com

And Thereafter...

If it was the end of the world today,
I'd dance with you till the end of my breath,
I'd say,turning into ice or burning in fire,
I'd kiss you like it was my only desire.
If we were to die,
We wouldn't die alone,
Our souls united, two skeletons, two bodies,
But I'd breathe in your bones.
Some may live through,
Some may perish in vain,
And if I were to live and you were to go,
You'd continue to live through my sorrow.
So, I'd rather perish along with you;
Dancing and dazzling in the chaotic hue.
I'd have life in my eyes,
Sparkling joy on my lips,
In the world of chaos, destruction amidst.
And thereafter we'd continue to live,
Together,
Forever,
No separation only bliss..

- Pratima
ID: pratimakolekar77@gmail.com

My Soulmate

In a world full of heartbreak;
Where millions of people meet and separate,
I was lucky enough to find my perfect mate.
His love was the ointment to all my pain,
His presence was enough to reduce my strain,
The definition of love
He did redesign and reframe.
In the ups and downs,
In the goods and bad,
He was by my side when I was sad.
In laughter and tears,
In mood swings when I get mad,
To give me love
That you always had.
To those who say that miracles don't take place,
I would like to show world your sweet face.
You are my ultimate happiness
Which i'll never misplace,

-Foram Dhawal Vora
ID: foram.shah1094@gmail.com

Showers

Sometimes you have to dig deep,
And yet, it could just be dry.
A belief, firm as rock,
There's more than what meets the eye.
Over the years, simmer beneath,
Mountain erupts, embers flied.
Dirt swallows the sun,
Light seems to have died.
Changes in the skies,
And behold the clouds have arrived.
The first drop vanished into vapour,
Sacrifices, but none greater.
Where the flowers fierce beautifully,
Bloom decades later.
From now the embers survive,
With fate for the showers to arrive.

-Iyherb
ID: clyndosuza@gmail.com

Mom To Be

Mumma is the word I would recall
when in trouble,
In few days I shall have my baby
who will bathe with bubble.
The baby shall be my sunshine in the day and my
dreams at night,
Little one shall look upto me
To understand difference in wrong and right.
There is a medley of emotions
Running in my mind,
Really! My Baby, My Angel will be of my kind?

Now, I wish to imbibe more good qualities
And values in me,
As in all the situations of life
My baby will learn from what it will see.
That feeling of giving up on own happiness
For baby's smile,
That Indirect explanations & examples
To improvise it's profile,
That unlimited concern & care
For its health & growth all while,
That proud feeling on its achievement
By putting an extra mile,
I am already excited by visualising
All of the above in its own style.
Feeling of being it's mother will make pains,

Cramps, vomits & the whole process worthwhile.

Little kicks remind me to have food on time,
Those body movements remind me
To take a break and sing a hymn.
My cravings make me think
Of what it would love to bite,
Attention of my friends and family on me
Is suddenly on hike.
It's a beautiful and exciting new phase of my life,
Where I would be upgraded to a responsible
mother from an understanding wife.

-CA Sruchi Pratik Dadia
ID: dadia.sruchi@gmail.com

The Emotions Talk

I hope!

I hope, you wouldn't change
Your feelings for me.
I hope, people's judgement
Wouldn't have clouded your opinion.
Not a word I could have said,
Change the way you felt.
Not a word you said,
Change the pain I had.
But, I hope stars align,
Two broken souls drifted apart,
Bringing us together!

-Nidhi Shah
ID: nidhishah1920.ns@gmail.com

Before I Die

Oh Death! When you come to me dear,
I want to call all my loved ones near.
Just give me that much of time,
Before I hear, my life's final hymn.
When the call from above would ring,
And my life will take that last swing,
Only one wish I have, I want one thing,
No one cries, only God's name they sing.
Every eye seeing me, will pour that rain,
But please! Let me go without any pain.
Lovingly you all give me that last farewell,
For your warmth will make me feel so well!
I have to go very far, closing my Life's file.
So, why not bid good bye, with a last smile?
Parting from you all, is a dreadful fear,
In your eyes, I just can't see a tear.
So before going on my longest date,
Last time, let me just see my mate.
"Death! Please, will you for sometime wait?"

But "No!" it said, perhaps that's our fate!
So now 'before I die', I promise you,
I'll never ever, alone leave you,
Just so that, we never ever part.
Like sweet memories,
I'll forever stay in your heart!

-Priyanka Doshi
ID: priyanka.matalia@gmail.com

Solitude

Surrounded by four walls,
Feeling helpless in this narrow, confined space.
My biggest fear was slowly turning into a reality,
With no way out my heart began to race.
There is an arched door,
One just around the corner.
Although, every time I reached for the knob
A stranger fear took over me, making me falter.
I walked around aimlessly
On the smoothly polished floor,
Yet it seemed to creak with every movement
Why? I'm quite unsure.
I sat down and glanced around,
The walls showcased an emotion-
A war of colors, both red and blue
Harmonized to create a subtle lilac hue.
I began to feel lonely, just like blue.
For when I am added to a color,
I'll make something new
But what will make me? I began to wonder.
I look outside the sealed window,
Giving smiles, waving to the world.
No one seemed to reciprocate,
Except my own reflection.
My heart burned.
Everything looked beautiful outside.

Birds chirping in the radiant sky,
Hearty laughter of blooming friendships
I wish I could go out, I sighed.
I felt weightless and friendless
Like a howling wind,
Wishing for a moment without brutality.
For my misery to not be a reason to grin,
Hoping to be welcomed,
With a little congeniality.
I wished for someone on the other side,
To show me that kindness is not unknown.
Someone who would open
That arched door for me
Saying, "It's okay to be scared,
You're not alone."

-Lubhani Goyal
ID: lubhanigoyal19@gmail.com

Imagine

Imagine a world with no borders, no guns,
No tanks no suicide bombers,
A world which is safe for
Our mothers, sisters and daughters,
A world where everyone's human,
No thought of slaughter.
Imagine a world with no religion, no hate,
No crime, just love and affection.
A world free of unwilling division,
A world where not society
But people take their own decisions.
Imagine a world with no aggression,
No pointless deaths, no need of protection.
A world where soldiers are also human
And not just defence, without emotions.
A world where their lives matter
And so do their relations.
Imagine a world with love,
A world where everyone is equal
None below, None above.

A world where everything is peaceful
Not just doves,
Because in front of humanity all hatred bows.
But yet again just IMAGINE.

-Prateek Dwivedi
ID: pruv28.09.15@gmail.com

Stories Inked

Though temporary it seems,
It sounded like a forever.
Caging themselves in, to save one another.
Country after country they all were counting.
Slowly it's taking each one down,
Turning those rumours into reality.
Through miles I can hear those thousand cry,
Pleading inside for this to stop
Questioning when will this all end?
Where for some lives were lost,
For some their daily living was on stake.
Family seeing their kids cry,
As their condition was worsening.
Many came raising their hands for help,
By all means they wanted to save.
For once no country, no caste,
No gender equality was on stake.
This made God say laughingly,
"Can a disease make you all one,
Was that all it took?"

Deep inside he too was filled with much of pain,
After seeing his kids suffer in vain.
Sooner or later this will all end,
And it will become a part of our history.
Some stories would start
How they survived through this,
Some stories would end with emotions inked!

-Divya Bora
ID: divyabora9@gmail.com

Darkness

I used to wonder,
Why the sun burns with so much intensity
And then disappears in darkness day after day.
Even on gloomy days it continues to spread light
And give everything life.
I used to wonder,
Why the moon shines at night,
Guiding everyone who needs light.
She is the mistress of the night,
She waxes and wanes,
And still continues to shine in pale light.
I used to wonder,
Why stars shine so bright?
Even in darkest night,
Until they perish to fulfil someone's wish
And then I realized that's what we humans do.
For someone we love
We give our everything
Until, we are lost in darkness forever

-Tanishka Khushlani
ID: tanishka555@gmail.com

A Dream To Remember

I turned 60 today.
All this time, exposed to pain,
Now when I'm old, I still feel the same.
Pain, I suppose got the most of me.
People flying with
Their expensive planes all around me,
And, I'm still sitting here on this rocking chair,
That I bought for my dad
When he had grey hair.
Letting the clock sit tight on the cracky wall,
Staring at it and hearing the tick tock.
This numbness that I feel now is not my age,
But my soul which was once red and now it's
beige.
I just wait for the cuckoo to pop out every hour,
To see my colour and give me a beautiful flower.
The books, the clocks everything is so rusty,
They are tangled with
Web and my heart stitched,
Problems overpowering my success,
Stealing the happiness from
Fate and magnifying the stress.
But, I'm still here smiling with my sweetheart,
Who stood beside me even when I didn't have a
head start.

I woke up!
Kissed my mom and dad good morning,
Laughing with my brother on pity issues,
Loving my friends and my darling,
Looked up at the heaven,
Thanking for the love, clothes and the shoes.
I turned 21 today,
All this time, I wasn't exposed to pain,
I was gifted with a meaning of life in a frame.

-Sangramjith Mukherjee
ID: mukherjeesangramjith@gmail.com

Bounded

Nothing rests in peace,
All the delights gone,
The place around amiss,
Making me anything but shone.
How will I do it? Without support?
I need the wings of care,
Of belonging as mare.
Peeping through the high walls,
I sort the clumsy weather,
Eyes spotting those malls,
Leaving sparkling eyes that matter.
I long to get some caress,
The freedom to fly,
To look world from my eyes,
To overcome the shy.
But here I am,
Locked inside the tower,
Nothing to kneel on,
Holding the gaze of star.
Wiping away the tears,
I gently try to calm my soul,
Walking as if it is just a gear,
Just when it wants to haul.

-Bhavya Gupta
ID: bhavya13994@gmail.com

Nostalgia

I commemorate your existence,
Through these fine drops so heavenly.
These drops, lingering on my skin,
Oh! how they touch me so tenderly.
Your touch was similar to these droplets-
So pure, so good, so tingling.
Aiming every inch of my body and soul,
So warm and comforting.
You're right here in these beautiful drops,
Quenching my thirst
Under this unconditional flow.
Washing away my ugly yesterday,
Blessing me today with this glow.
I relive you in these showers.
These showers so cold but yet so warm.
I relive your touch in these running waters,
But like these drops,
You're here one second and then,
You're gone.

-Chrislyn Dsouza
ID: clyndosuza@gmail.com

Monotony! Monotony!

I reach my college,
Remove the earphones off my ears,
Roll them off, crumble them in my pocket,
I take the stairs nowadays
For, the elevators just feel a more reluctant.
I reach the fifth floor,
Wish the watchman a good day,
And enter the class.
This, is a whole new world,
With multiple personalities.
From oppressed activists,
To classy toppers.
From happy families,
To depressed loners.
You'll find them all,
Strained in a classroom.
I ignore them all,
And quietly sit on the second last seat.
For the last, is too scary
Of my own incompetence or the zeal.
I take out my earphones,
Down my head and, just zone out.
Until, one loud guy comes asking
About stuffs totally unrelated.
Relented, I enter the washroom,
Throw my earphones back into the pocket,

Splash some water and then,
Regain my senses that,
This is not gonna stop.
However life I wished for,
This has to be my future.
For, many well-wishers want me to do this.
This time, I enter a class with some enthusiasm.
High-five the front benchers,
Pat on the guy ahead of me.
Crack some mildly offensive jokes
And constantly smile.
But as soon as I get out of the place,
I walk slow.
I put my earphones on,
This time, all that plays, is black silence.
They tell me, overhearing is a crime,
But not when you aren't able
To listen to yourself.
I get back home,
Lock myself in my room,
Have a mint tablet,
Throw my phone on the bed.
Now, tears don't stop,
Neither do I want them to.
My chest feels heavy,
Not because of the inherent weight
That I've gained,
But, something surely doesn't feel right. I cry.

I let the dried rose in my novel
Peel it's petals and smell them.
They smell of broken dreams.
Who knows, that rose might have been wanting
Some soil to let the sorrows bury or to grow.
And was plucked by a nasty human
To beautify the novel.
That rose has cried, inside pages,
Begotten it's thorns and it's fragrance.
But now, before moving out of the room,
I keep another rose inside the book.
And I smile. I smile again.
And live the life that has been given to me.
The next day, I reach my college,
Remove the earphones,
Roll them off, crumble them in my pocket....

-Rutuparn Kulkarni
ID: rutuparn2010@gmail.com

Ode To The Waves

Your flow inundates the sun,
Only for a sight so magical.
The bright sun stops dazzling,
But alleviates my soul.
The evenings around you
Have vanquished my fight with anxiety.
The mortals doesn't see,
That the hopes hanging in the nightfall
Are bought by you.
Slowly the hope keeps falling on my feet
Piercing my soul to stitch with the freedom
Only to release this edifice of bones
And flesh from this manumission.

-Himadri Gogoi
ID: himadrigogoi1693@gmail.com

A Dream Or Nightmare

If I had guts to stop you for a while
The distance between us
Wouldn't have reached miles.
The days I remember when we were one soul.
The love for which our times we stole.
When we were there just away a dial
But now we are poles separated by a mile.
I still remember the night
When your breaths were deep,
Our hugs were tight with an adrenaline leap.
With every moment our gaps were reduced,
The boundaries of love were all set loose.
With entangled souls and lips a bit apart,
Indeed it was the night of an alluring start.
But now I think it was just a dream,
A beautiful nightmare which makes me scream.

-Rishabh Chaube
ID: rishabhchaube96@gmail.com

Broken Was Okay!

When I wake up in the morning,
Wanting to sleep more.
Or maybe not wanting to wake up
Or maybe feeling that the darkness
Of the eyes closed are comforting,
You told me that broken was okay.

When I went to work with a smiling face
And suddenly when the smile turns blank,
Blank to watching only the collagen floaters,
Blank to feeling
The blood rushing in my stomach,
Blank to realise that
My body temperature is rising,
To the degree of my failure and pain,
You told me that broken was okay.

When you found me afraid to believe-
Believe in the words of people around me,
Believe that my ambitions are not gone,
Because I don't feel motivated about them,
Believe that I am capable
Of achieving what I dreamt of,
You told me that broken was okay.

When you saw the fear-
Fear to love the people around me,
Fear to be going through
The rollercoaster of hustle,
Fear to be vulnerable,
You told me that broken was okay.

And when you told me that broken was okay,
I knew I could sleep a little more around you,
I knew I could be a little blank with you,
I knew I could believe in you,
I knew I could fear around you,
And you would still be okay!

-Shivani Gole
ID: rtr.shivani.gole@gmail.com

Unseen Pain

Her agony was deeper
Than the wounds on body,
Her pain was one of those that had no heal..
There were no emotions which she could feel..
As fear was the one she couldn't deceive..
When she tried to mend
Those wounds with the ray of hope,
The memories of her past haunted her and Made
her revoke.
Those screams, those words
Unexpressed unspoken,
She couldn't find a place of comfort or solace..
As he touched not just the body but also her
emotion that were fragile,
She had no option but
Just to rise up strong and agile.
Her body was touched in a inevitable way,
And she hardly had a word to utter,
When the hand mend to mentor;
Did made her shatter.

No part of her BODY was left untouched,
The person she loved
Just used her to fulfill his lust.
Every part of her soul still feels the pain,
Will she ever be able to get rid of the stain?

-Foram Dhawal Vora
ID: foram.shah1094@gmail.com

Parted Ways

The days were longer when I thought about you,
Every second seemed like an hour to me.
The rising sun reminded me of a happy you,
And the shinning moon
Gave me glimpses of a contended you.
Morning dew touched my skin,
Just like your soft fingers.
And the whistling wind
Made my thoughts shiver.
And then the hard reality strikes,
Making me realize of the hardened vibes,
That you and me are no longer.
You living your own life
And me mine.

-Akshaya Bandivdekar
ID: rtr.akshaya@gmail.com

Our Own Self

For Me

Deep I see someone close,
Deeper is the love I find for her,
Deepest is the hidden feelings for her!
For the last I remember,
She didn't felt the same for me.
Where I made her feel happy at every moment,
It took just a second for her to break me apart.
Do you remember the blossoms
Of the eastern express highway
During the month of March?
Early morning at 6 we met,
I took you there, a long drive full of emotions.
Those beautiful white and pink flowers and
Those windy breeze you felt on your face,
The sunshine that made you hide behind me,
Didn't they make you feel for me?
I held your hand tight
Until you were back smiling,
Walking together ahead of vain.
And it just took you a minute to leave me,
And go back to him again?
Does he even know, you cried the whole night,
Scribbling your hand with blood?
Does he even know you love pink roses
Without sprinkled water droplets?

And you still went back to him,
Without thinking a second about me.
Lost is the every feeling now,
Lost is the love that my heart had for you.
Lost is my smile which you admired a lot.
Lost is the Aman you know!
How do I say that key to my heart is lost?
How do I say the key to my smile has changed?
How do I say Aman you know is estranged?
For every passing minute
Is admiring you in my dreams,
The way you look at me and I at you,
Is there something for me you feel?

-Amanjeet
ID: m.amanjeet.s@gmail.com

Life Of A Woman

Love is a word so complicated to define,
But with woman, it's delicate and fine!
With her heart, in abundance she gives,
It's in her soul, and that's how she lives!

When she is a child, it's meaning is simple,
Love for her is mom's kisses in ample.
From dad she gets hugs innumerable.
With siblings, her childhood is memorable!

And then slowly, she enters in her teens,
When within rises, waves of love umpteen.
Confused but cheerful is the state of mind,
That's a funny love, one of its kind.

Then came twenties, an important age,
Where love and desire, are all at its rage.
An independent working girl,
Breaking all norms,
Happily, she is living life,
On her own sweet terms.

Suddenly one day,
He comes and holds her hand,
Her marital dreams come true, with a big band.

She is now a wife, for family a daughter-in-law,
She has to fulfill all her duties, without any flaw.

He's always there to hold her from falling,
Love now means, his support
And understanding.
His love always make her worries to flee,
He stands by her side, that brings her glee!

Then one fine day, good news comes flying in,
Which heralds a hope,
Her transformation within.
They welcome their child, happily together.
She is now complete; she is a Mother!

Love and Life, both get a new meaning.
For, in her child she sees a new beginning.
Happiness now means, her child's lovely smile,
For which she will boldly cross, all extra miles.

Love keeps growing, as her child grows.
Success and happiness, for her child unfolds.
Her child gets married and life takes a turn,
Now to her life, a new leaf will upturn.

Love now means, her child happily united,
With everyone together, her family completed.
She now gradually passes, all her values ahead,

So that in her family, there's never any dread!

Now she is old, she has become a "granny,"
With new generation, coping up is a tyranny.
But wobbling words make it so easy,
She was retired, but now again so busy!

Love continues from generation to generation,
But time has come today for the last narration.
With her loved ones, gathered around her bed,
Love now means, to cherish old times instead!

In her husband's lap,
She closes her eyes peacefully,
His touch on her forehead, made her go joyfully.
Satisfaction from her life, that was her love.
She flew away very far, like a white dove!

-Priyanka Doshi
ID: priyanka.matalia@gmail.com

Conversation

She was sitting in the balcony
With her favorite cup of coffee
And her all time favorite novel.
He came and looked at her.
"Evening gorgeous!"
Broke the silence by greeting her
and asking,"Why'd you choose me?"
She put her mug and put that novel aside,
Looked at him in the eyes and said
"Because you were looking out of the metro
instead of your phone"

-Komal Verma
ID: vermakomal47470@gmail.com

You Are Enough

Wake up,
Look in the mirror,
Tell yourself,
"Good Morning Beautiful"
You don't need any text
To feel that.
You are enough.

-Coco
ID: cocotales47@gmail.com

Her

Oh my god,
Have you ever seen this beautiful thing?"
She said startlingly.
"Damn! I can sit here all day,"
She kept talking.
There was twinkle in her eyes
And much brighter face,
Because of the sunset,
His because of her.

-Coco
ID: cocotales47@gmail.com

Loving Your Own Kind

I was searching for happiness,
But all I felt was the emptiness.
Each day passed by,
With me looking down upon myself,
They convinced me of the fact
That I needed help.
Every night the river of my emotions flowed,
Was it a crime to love your own kind?
You came in my life
When I needed you the most,
On this, I would like to raise a toast.
You marked the beginning
To the journey of my acceptance,
For now, I care less about my appearance.
You were the big change of my life,
You are the one who saved me
From stabbing myself with a knife.
Earlier I wished I could be like others.
But no more, you've made me realize,
Love is blind,
And it is not wrong to love your own kind.

-Samriddhi Agrawal
ID: samriddhi2810@gmail.com

My External Cocoon

My stygian skin binds the bone and flesh
beneath,
These jet threads bind my carapace,
The constant source of my humiliation,
Pains my aureate soul,
whose allure is unable to dazzle any.
My cotton candy frame which rolls around the
bony cage,
Fluffy enough to enchant all,
The constant source of my humiliation,
Pains my aureate soul,
whose allure is unable to dazzle any.
The society puts tags on me,
I ain't clothes that need to be of perfect fit,
I ain't home decor that needs to be of measured
perfection,
I am a human of flesh and bone,
being with feelings and emotions,
My real beauty lies in the butterfly within.
Why doesn't my soul's golden allure dazzle the
hollow society,
just like it does to me?

-Pratyusha Bhattacharjee
ID: bubun27699@gmail.com

Mother Knows Best

Fellow humans, we called for this,
Before which our lives were a total "bliss!"
Our busy selves, slaves to commitments,
Knew nothing beyond faking diligence!
We received warnings, were given signs,
Until our mother drew the line!
Now she reminds us of her younger self,
As she demands to spend time with herself!
Her laughter during the roaring winds,
Dawn light sheer up to the birds that sing!
The animals, once captivated,
Are out of the fence,
She asks us to remain indoors, hence.
Her children, though, always in a quarrel,
For whom will they blame for another's evil!
They now see a mother, shed her tears,
For once, after ages, she's gotten all their ears,
Her complains are many with endless fears!

How long will it take for us to know,
That our mother has never needed us more!
She has given us plenty and expected very little,
But fools were we, with hearts so brittle!

It's time we stand by her,
Nourish, cherish, and let love shower,
For, there will be a time when she will perish,
No economy will matter then,
Except the times with her
That we have cherished!

-Dhritti Shah
ID: shahdhritti@gmail.com

Sounds Of Silence

It was a dark night when we first encountered,
You were to my rescue when I was floundered.
I sat on the bench gawking at a star,
Wondering how did it all turn bizarre?
I closed my eyes and sank deep into thoughts,
Just when one voice broke out into talks.
The voice sounded familiar,
The thoughts were intimate,
It looked like God was here to run my fate.
"This too shall pass, good days are on your way,
You're worthy of all, don't let it downfall."
Said the voice as firm as an ice.
I opened my eyes to the illuminating shine,
In a blink, I start to whine.
The voice was gone,
My superpower was withdrawn.
I looked around in the
Glow of moonlight serenade,
Unleashing the knowledge of the escapade.
The one who was loud enough to be around,
Was now nowhere to be found.
I sat there desperately waiting for it to return,
Longing to hear the things it made me learn.
I close my eyes again, this time to pray,
Begging it to come back in any way.

"Don't let the hard times break you,
Don't let your skies turn grey.
Don't cry in despair, you're unique and rare.
Get up and hit the road,
It's your time to explode.
And I opened my eyes with
No fear of losing the sound,
For now I know from
Where the sound was pronounced.
The sound which resided in me,
Yet constricted in me.
The sound where communicating
Needs no talking.
The sound where my darkness
Meets my brightness.
The sound from within that has always been in.
The sound of guidance,
The sound of my silence."

-Saniya More
ID: moresaniya@gmail.com

Appreciate

Why limit yourself to the mind and body?
Why even limit it to the feelings in our hearts?
Your spirit and energy are capable of things,
Beyond imagination.
Let your soul connect with the universe around.
The universe has different weathers,
But you always want it to be sunny.
It's okay if things are not rosy all the time.
It's okay to feel down and weary.
There's a night and there's a day.
One incomplete without the other.
If you achieve to love both,
The light and the dark within you,
You have never known love better.
Let your soul pour out to the universe.
Let the energies sync and be one.
Let's not crave for desires anymore.
Let's not keep high expectations within.
Explore your capabilities,
Explore the unsurpassed.
Cherish every emotion that comes with it.
Appreciate every day like it's your last.
Swim through the energies of the world.
Float under the reflections of the sky.

Cherish the view from down below,
Appreciate the universe up high.
Walk on the paths put of your league.
Stride till you reach your goal.
Cherish the failures on the way,
Appreciate your learning soul.

-Chrislyn Dsouza
ID: clyndosuza@gmail.com

Mother

Always in search of that happy place,
I walked this path for years.
Unintentionally we all have it,
As we follow our peers.

And when I found it by mistake,
I was struck with awe.
It was not some beach or some lake,
This place; I could not even fathom or draw.

In this polluted world she was the cleanser
As she always showed you the way.
Protecting the family and her,
Like a queen on chessboard;
Keeps everyone at bay.

She always gave the wisest advice,
And showed resilience for what like offered.
To feed her children
She would give up her bread slice,
Mother!
A good gentleman in me you hammered.

-Aniket Naik
ID: aniket.naik@yahoo.in

Dear "YOU"

Rejecting every dirt pile,
You give me reasons to smile.
Forgetting all the grim,
You teach me not to let my shine dim.
Instead of panicking on loss,
You make me embrace each side of a toss.
From leaving everything incomplete
With rejection,
You motivate me to complete with perfection.
From the state of getting tired,
You give my heart strength to not get retired.
You turned an angry hellfire
To an ocean of desire
From irritating and mocking,
You've left no door unlocking my heart's depth.
You make me achieve everything from nothing.
You stayed with me in harmony all through,
Just like my organs do.
Although, you're not my boyfriend or husband,
Still you love me the most
And make me feel at home.
Along with blood, you flow in my veins.
Without you, my life is vain.

As, you're the first beam of sunshine
That makes its way
Through the corners of the window.
To wake me up in the morning
You're the first cup of tea
That keeps me refreshed throughout the day.
You're the first drizzle of showers
That drifts my laziness away.
In the world full of
Fakeness and broken promises,
You're eternally here to stay.
Dear Constant!
To thank you there may be ways,
Some few, but let me just conclude by saying I
LOVE YOU.

-Debalina De
ID: debalinade2@gmail.com

Secrets

Oh God this freedom,
It's the greatest sin I possess.
Freedom to feel, is my grandest weakness.
Nevertheless, charm me to heaven
I shall gaily be sent,
Oh, the odour of your presence
Is enough to entice my addiction.
Purity is the burning devil,
Darling save me from his flames.
Carry me to the Lord,
Let him take my fire away.
Oh sweetheart so naive,
Push through your narrow mind,
Capture the love through my eyes,
You might see the love I outlined.

-Akshaya Iyer
ID: rtrakshayaiyer99@gmail.com

Kaleidoscope And Concrete

When he asks you
If you notice the little things about him,
He's not talking about the romance
In untied shoelaces or melted ice-creams.
He's wondering about his wrists
And the way he organizes his music collection.
She doesn't.
And I know she doesn't.
I am familiar with the feeling
Of having skin painted by crying wasted days
And a youth stolen
By aching muscles and leaking blood.
I can read the thoughts
In your head at this moment:
Why will she save you?
Who will be interested in the fine art
Of your bullshit or fifty shades of your blood?
But hey, open your heart just a little.
She might have failed to see the marks,
But she does enquires you
If you got home okay,
And she does ask you to get some sleep.
I do offer you some of my fries.
Isn't that love?

I'm not trying to demean your pain in any way,
But I need to send across this reminder:
The laughter from your tombstone
Will haunt us forever.
And its smallest coffins
That weigh the heaviest on our chests.
Please don't think that
God will save you from this.
I've seen the old gods dying and
I don't have the heart to see
The same happening to you.
We understand the loneliness of insomnia and
The loneliness of
An accomplishment go unnoticed,
But if that is what it takes,
We pray that
The accomplishment we never notice
Was how the tears of blade
Was an offer you refused this time.
I'm sorry that I fail to perceive you sometimes,
And she's sorry too –
But spin us, speak to us about your struggles
And we will write you letters
And bung in handmade paper dolls
And small bubblegum with pressed flowers.
I know the entire universe is in an uninterrupted
Black and white every once in a while.

But please adjust
Your microscope lens moderately,
It's kaleidoscopic, this was just one round.
The poetries which taught
That you've to be prepared for war
If you want peace is crap,
And I'll show you how to be at peace
With yourself w/o raging those wars.
1. Finish your crossword puzzle.
2. Feed the ducks.
3. Wear stretchy pants
4. Cookies - always cookies and five,
I hope this reached you on time.
Also, I just read somewhere today that
You're iron and you reek rust
And that the human thigh bone is stronger than
concrete.

-Hemali Gandhi
ID: rtr.hemaligandhi@gmail.com

Society

Love For Lust

He nurtured her with love,
But valued only her anatomy.
He treated her like a queen,
But only when she was nude in the scene.
She cheered, her soul was in fear,
She believed, her soul was in grief.
His time for her was a boon,
But for him, hormones were fortune.
To be with him was her dream,
But for him she was a human barbie
To act in his film.

-Rtr. Sarmila Chakraborty
ID: chakrabortysharmila604@gmail.com

STOP

And after loosing so many people,
Who you thought would stay forever?
We stopped expecting that
From new people,
Because we know
They might not
And maybe us too.

-Komal Verma
ID: vermakomal47470@gmail.com

Grow More Trees

Let's pause and reflect at the days gone by.
The lock down has been tough,
But honestly when did u notice last, a bird fly?
CORONA has made us stop and think
Of all things we take for granted without a blink!
This earth is what we owe to nature,
Let's preserve for our generations later.

-Partha Vidhani
ID: parthavidhani@hotmail.com

To All Who Gave Up

One day...
Someone will come and
Make you believe in love again,
Someone will come and
Make you feel beautiful again,
Someone will come and
Make you feel special again,
Someone will come and make you happy again ,
Someone will come and make you believe,
That how breathtaking you look
When u smile again.
Someone will come and make you believe,
How bright your face looks
When you wake up in the morning again,
Someone will come and make you believe
How cute are late night video calls again,
Someone will come and make you believe
All things are precious
Which you forgot and thought were fake.

-Coco
ID: cocotales47@gmail.com

Drug Abuse

My first time as I recall,
was with my friends in my late teens.
The first puff made me cough,
The second set me free.
It didn't take much time
To go from cigarettes to marijuana.
Haunted my peer pressure and encouraged by
"kuch nai hoga chill maarna."
Those snorts during lectures,
Exhaling smoke rings after college.
Now, I, remorseful in corners
Neck taped with nicotine bandage.
Ruined my youth
In shameful activities of "getting high"
Running after temporary elated moments of joy.
Now, I wish I had worked hard on my career,
Made my parents say, "That's MY BOY!"
My own daughter had always refrained
From watching a movie
With me making excuses,
I wondered why?
Finally one day we watched a movie
And it wasn't MUKESH who embarrassed her,
But her own father who made her cry.

I see these youngsters loitering
In the middle of the night.
Eyes are red, stumbling in walks,
Alcohol is inside.
Had I stopped this earlier,
Never continued these cheap thrills.
I'd be happily paying my house taxes
And not these hospital bills.
I hope someone treading the same road
Reads this,
Understands that this regret
Makes me wish I were dead.
Luckily, doctor said I've only got
A few hours to live,
But my wife's wailing with a face so red.
These activities are cloaked under "Recreational,"
Don't fall for the illusion.
The person just needs right direction and help,
This is the perfect solution.

-Pranav Diya
ID: pranavkdiya@gmail.com

Poverty

I'm a boy from Mumbai, living in a slum.
Where's "DEMOCRACY!"
Just politics full of scum.
Poverty is not a phase, it's an appalling state.
I can't afford new books,
So I rewrite on the black slate.
It's funny how people look at us
In disgust and turn around.
Themselves being the one
Who bury black money underground.
From afternoon to evening,
I work at the tea stall by the station.
I return home just to see
My younger brother dying due to starvation.
My mother sings me to sleep every night.
Sees my burnt hands,
Hides her tears from my sight.
No one's here to listen to the voices of the streets.
Society's fragmented into
"Classes""Hierarchy" and "Creed."
Every five years, they'll come with new
And bigger fake promises.
"24 hours water," and "Hygienic premises."
My mother is a menial housemaid,
Works in her employer's bungalow.

Suffering through the predicaments
My granny says, "go with the flow."
We don't have the monetary resources
To bring justice to our people who are wronged.
So we influence through our poems, speeches,
Some of us via our songs.
I see rich kids enjoying their childhood
On the playground.
Eyes burning with anticipation,
Wishing to turn my life around.
They will make movies and documentaries
About us to entertain.
But no one's helping to improve this livelihood,
While we cry in disdain.
We work day and night drenched in sweat.
Return home to sleep on the footpath
Which is our bed.
Somebody save us from this hell hole
And uplift our life.
Lend a helping hand whenever you can,
Let humanity thrive!

-Pranav Diya
ID: pranavkdiya@gmail.com

It's Okay

The world is crumbling,
But it's okay, really, it's okay.
Economies are stalled,
Socializing appalled,
All Gods being called,
But it's okay, really, it's okay.
Go, with families & self cherish.
Go, let all differences perish.
Go, applause the heroes in relish.
For it's okay, really, it's okay.

-ReyHan
ID: sshreyang@gmail.com

Kashmir Is A Woman

Ah, that look, the one that
You're giving me right now.
Your eyes scream, "Stay silent, Stay hush."
Your head frowns, you clench your fist.
I've spilled a secret, I suppose.
I will hold my head up high,
Be eye to eye,
With your god and mind.
'Kashmir is a woman' Don't ask me why.
The struggle starts from where the Jhelum flows.
In that sacred valley,
Where the birds sing sad songs,
Stood a woman, heavily clothed with shame.
She wrapped her newborn daughter, in a cloth,
Which was as white as the snow
That was leaving no place
For the child in the newly dug grave.
Unnamed, she left the world and
Granted her father his much deserved honour.
The mother's cry is a song
The birds have adopted.
They sing it, throughout the valley
And relief is restored.
A rape is prevented.

"I want to grow up and be like papa"
These words sting the heart of a mother,
A wife who lost her husband,
To the desire of his so called freedom.
Enslaved she is, with work that bends her bone,
Her will to survive is found low.
She has yet to put
Her master's leftover food on her child's plate.
There's work that demands her
To fulfill the monstrous desire of men
That possibly killed her husband.
Don't get her wrong.
Don't you dare bat an eye at her.
They say the roof is enormous,
Her dignity is little.
But she is just a mother,
Trying to stop her son
From becoming like his father.
Draped in red, the chadar on her head,
The bindi on her forehead.
Her crimson lips break in a smile,
When her mother says,
Your mehendi has gotten dark with time.
Weddings in Kashmir, you see,
Are filled with hope and certainty.
It's one of the few times,
When someone knocks on your door
And you know why.

Your cupboard changes
To vibrant colours from white.
You hope, you hope,
For the groom to arrive,
With roses in his hand
When he slides down from the mare.
In their claps and drumbeats,
You want to forget the cries of yesterday.
He will arrive, won't he?

-Mariam Lakdawala
ID: mariamlakdawala8@gmail.com

Lockdown - Beating The Virus

Wondering when will the sun shine on my face,
The air flowing through her tresses.
But had to rush home
Before the police could chase,
Stay indoors the government stresses.

Before a drug is found,
Need to confide in this isolation.
Inside my home I'm bound,
Counting food & ration.

This war we have to win,
Economies slowing; falling of nations.
This pandemic has put everyone in their bin,
As this biological threat was in creations.

From the belly of a bat,
When humans contracted.
This virus they hath,
Disruption it caused;
Human eye cannot have refracted.

Let's stay alone & fight,
For this is a battle not for us.
For future generations
Stay peacefully they might,
For our kids or grandparents;
Stay without any fuss.

-Aniket Naik
ID: aniket.naik@yahoo.in

What's With The Girl?

What's with the girl
And her smile?
My granny told me not to show my teeth
It attracts Malice!!

What's with the girl
And her smile?
My teacher told me not to smile
As I have the most crooked teeth!!
What's with the girl
And her smile?
My lover told me not to show the curve
It's like I want to bed others!!

What's with the girl
And her smile?
My husband said why not?
Always grim and stern!!

What's with the girl
And her smile?
Nothing she just wants to decide
When can and when not to SMILE!!

-Swetha Ponnekanti
ID: ponnekanti.swetha@gmail.com

He Touched Me With His Eyes

I was walking my path and suddenly
He touched me with his eyes.
I complained but couldn't argue,
They said he didn't do wrong.
Yet I feel insecure,
Since he did touch me with his eyes.
I dodged, ran away but his eyes followed.
I told this to people
But no one listened,
As he only touched me with his eyes.
I wanted to stay home locked
But couldn't deny my vigour to stand out.
One day I lashed on him
And he ran away far
But next day
There were another set of eyes.

-Avani Yadav

The Wedding Night

My road was straight and clear,
But you were my knight
In shining armour that made me fear.
The deformity in your cheeks made me weak.
The closer you drew,
The more my fear grew.
Those eyes of yours had now ran dry,
I wondered if I could stay a little longer
And make you, your favourite omelette fry.
They said you have to go once you were called.
But I know the promises that you recall.
Till death May do us apart
Was what I said,
But you had promised
To protect me till your last breath.
Yet, you stayed there standing like a fool
When your wife called me a slut
And killed me till my body became cool.
Was it my fault to love you
Even when you had tied a knot?
You were the one supposedly at fault.
But I was buried
For standing by someone I loved a lot.

Now I know why your eyes had dried
Because you were awake
Trying to bury the evidence that night.
I will be waiting for you in that bright light
Which you called upon on me
On the disastrous wedding night.

- Vijaylaxmi
ID: vijaylaxmi.gurav03@gmail.com

The Lump

Lump in my stomach how did you get in there
How is it that you disintegrated
The happiness of my life?
The showers of blessing turned into hails of fire.
The lump in my stomach
Leads to the lump in my throat.
But I shall not cry for
I've the burden of my family,
Their contentment lies in the state of my eyes.
My dry eyes make
Them think I'm strong enough,
I sigh knowing
They don't know the screaming inside me.
My hair fell down and
With that so does my spirit,
I wish if only I could fix one of them again.
My bald head makes me feel
Like a small baby again,
I think of it as I'm born again
After the hell I've been through.
Thousands of radiations
Pierce through my body,
Each one destroying
A thousand hopes inside me.
At times I give in
To the burning of the hope inside me,

At times I use it as a flame to fire me up.
I see the way people look at me
When they see my lump,
The silence of their mouth unable
Contain the sound of their eyes.
And, yet, I stand tall
Against the pity looks they fire at me.
For, they don't know that
I've come out of the radiation fired at me.
My cries of pain still haunt
The very existence of my body.
I still remember the way
Every fiber of my being disintegrated.
Once again it broke me down
To the mere ashes of my existence,
Only to see me rise again
From the ashes of certain death.
A lump in my stomach
Won't lead to a lump in my life.
I shall not let it dismantle the happiness
That remains I shall fight,
Fight a losing battle at times if I have to.
But I shall not give in
To the cries of pain inside me.

- Niket Joshi
ID: joshiniket50@gmail.com

To The Unheard Me, You And Everyone!

Yes I am unclear, just like
All of these thoughts in my mind,
Of all these memories that lie behind.
No, I am not going to dig inside,
Nor am I planning to look behind.
The hope of someone else
Liking me is much lesser now,
Because I am loving myself
The way I have derived,
Irrespective of the way
The world is going to look at me.
How I perceive myself is the key.
Yes, I know I am much more stronger now
And I am asked not to vent out.
But do you really think any beautiful change
Comes without feeling the stake of pain?
In this pretty world full of
Forged smiles and fictitious laughter
Can I be the one with a clear no?
A no for not lying,
A no for not faking,
A no for not saying something I do not feel?

I would rather say what I feel,
It maybe something good
Or something that maybe barbarous like hell.
If you think it's insane to say
Something that's in your mind?
It's probably because
You haven't treasured yourself enough.
Of all the things I have learnt,
Keeping oneself above is the key.
It is ensured that one day
We all will surely conquer the world.
But first let us learn to keep ourself
Above everyone else's thoughts and perception,
Because who we are has more to do with us
And less to do with them, less to do with them!

-Maitri Gada
ID: rtr.maitrigada@gmail.com

What Was Sent To The Soldier's Home?

From golden fields of Punjab?
From Punjab they got
A sack full of wheat
To grind and to eat.
Oh the sack full of wheat
From golden fields of Punjab.

What was sent to the soldier's home?
From Jaipur city of pink?
From Jaipur they got silver anklets
Thick they were and they flick.
Oh the anklets thick
From Jaipur city of pink.

What was sent to the soldier's home?
From sands of Jaisalmer?
From Jaisalmer they got
Spices so rare to cook and to share.
Oh the spices so rare
From sands of Jaisalmer.

What was sent to the soldier's home?
From Kutch the desert white?
From Kutch they got An embroidered shawl.

They framed in the hall
Oh the embroidered shawl,
From Kutch the desert white.

What was sent to the soldier's home?
From Aizawl the farthest east?
From Aizawl they got finest handpicked tea
They boiled it with glee.
Oh the handpicked tea
From Aizawl the farthest east.

What was sent to the soldier's home?
From the valley of Kashmir?
From Kashmir they got
Just a Tri-coloured shroud.
It made them so proud.
Oh the Tri-coloured shroud
From the valley of Kashmir.

-Abhishek Avhad
ID: abhishekavhad@gmail.com

Being A Man

Piece by piece you kill me each moment,
Whenever you talk about
Gender equality, sexual base,
Moral rights, etiquettes and so on.
Is it fair for this mother Earth
To not treat me motherly enough?
All because I am a man by birth
Who isn't sure about
The intensity of the pain of the womb?
I am asked not to solitude myself,
Being a man it's not my right.
And so if I am tough,
I am taught about other genders and their rights.
Okay, so being a male I am asked not to cry.
But, but, but, isn't it my right,
Whether it maybe to cry or to fly?
Or do the by laws only specify right
For one gender and not others?
I have been always helping my sisters
Whether it maybe about cooking
Or about looking after the household chores.
Don't I need someone to love me,
Not the same way as I do but at least half of it?

And if I find someone
Whom I can share my house with,
You give me the names of
Being a crap, a jerk and a monster,
Who is just there excitedly aroused all the time;
I agree there are some, yes there are some.
But can you please respect me
Just on the basis of who I am?
And not on the basis of my gender
Or the amount of money I have in my clutch!
'The feeling of him of being who he is.'

-Maitri Gada
ID: rtr.maitrigada@gmail.com

Rotaraction With Passion

The life of a Rotaractor is not an easy life.
It's an ocean of opportunities
Worth giving a dive.
The journey from becoming a member,
Is all that you'll remember!
Your development becomes
The center of every project,
You keep on improving
And upgrading your intellect.
You do every bit to serve the community,
It shows your generosity & your heart's purity!
Your professional development
Is all that happens in the flow,
Eventually your personality will outgrow.
Making you the leader the world needs now,
You become a person whom all want to endow!
Rotaract stands for Rotary-In-Action,
Your selection shows your ability & passion.
You become the person everyone admires,
You become the milestone that inspires!
The avenues in Rotaract are all essential,
Makes you a person influential.
Club Service Projects increases the bond,
Takes your friendship to a level beyond!
Sports Projects improves your endurance,
Makes you a person of great importance!

International Service Projects
Increases your network,
Helps you expand and showcase your effort.
Entrepreneurship Development is
What the world demands now,
You are the person who showcases to do it how!
Innovation & Communication are all required,
Making your position all acquired.
The Job of the Secretariat is not an easy work,
Dedication & Compassion
Symbolizes your mark.
The Documentation for every action,
Helps the organisation and
Showcases your education.
The President is the person worth appreciation,
The person with great love & affection!
Decision making abilities shows the dedication,
Observing every aspect with attention!
You must join this movement
That changes your life,
Makes you a person that strive.
Ending it with the dialogue
In the Rotaract fashion,
Let's Strive to Achieve with that ONE "Soch"
And Make It Happen!

-Vicky Gupta
ID: gupta.vicky.nk@gmail.com

Anokhi Thi Woh Baatein
Anokhe The Woh Din

Zindagi bhi kaise khwaab dekhati hai
Kabhi bachpan ke sapne toh
Kabhi pehla pyaar yaad dilati hai
Anokhi thi voh baatein anokhe the voh din
Jab dost parivaar sab sahi lagte the
Jab vishwas karna jurm nahi lagta tha
Jab logon ki rai chubhti nahi thi
Jab maa baap ke saath rehna aasan lagta tha
Jab teacher ki piche se chugli karte the
Jab lad jagad kar tiffin share karna padta tha
Jab exam ki padhai pure saal chalti thi
Jab pehle pyaar ka izhaar karna
Aasan nahi lagta tha
Anokhe thi voh baatein anokhe the voh din
Kaha kho jaate hai zindagi ki raftar mein
Ke bhul jaate hai aapno ko sansaar mein
Kaha kho jaate hai career ke piche
Ke bhul jaate hai bachpan ke sapne
Kaha kho jaate hai hookups ke chakkar mein
Ke bhul jaate hai barish mein
Pyaar ke izhaar karne
Aaj shayad aapse apne bachpan
Ki yaad dilana nahi aaya hu

Aaj shayad aapse apne maa baap ki
Yaad dilane nahi aaya hu
Aaj sirf voh asli insaan se milane aaya hu
Yeh dukh dard ego self respect ko kuch lamhon
ke liye juda karane aaya hu
Thode waqt ke liye zindagi kitni aasan hai
Yeh mehsoos karane aaya hu
Shayad nashe ke liye alcohol ya cigrate se pehle
khudko yaad dilane aaya hu
Ke bas anokhi thi voh baatein
Aur anokhe the tum yaad dilane aaya hu..

-Karan Mehta
ID: mehta.karan1998@gmail.com

कदर उनकी भी करो

कदर उनकी भी करो,

जो तुम्हे बिना मतलब के प्यार करता है !

कदर उनकी भी करो, जो तुम्हे दिल से चाहते है !

कदर उनकी भी करो,

जो तुम्हे बेवजह मोहब्बत करते है !

क्यूंकि, ऐसे लोग ख़ास नहीं, लेकिन कम है,

जिनका दिल नासमज है, लेकिन सच्चा है!

-Nidhi Shah
ID: nidhishah1920.ns@gmail.com

परेशान

यह कैसी असमंजस में पड़ गया हूँ मै?

अभी तक ज़िंदा हूँ या मर गया हूँ मै?

वो बक बक करता लड़का

आज नाउम्मीद इंसान हो गया है,

ये मन आज शांत नहीं बैठ रहा,

क्या करूँ परेशान हो गया है।

वो जिंदादिली की मिसाल,

आज दिल ज़िंदा है या नहीं पता नहीं।

आसमानों के जंजाल में कोई

आजाद परिंदा है या नहीं पता नहीं।

उन अकेली आखों से कह दो,

उनके लिए आँसुओं का इंतजाम हो गया है।

ये मन आज शांत नहीं बैठ रहा,

क्या करूँ परेशान हो गया है।

ईमान की क्या औकात है,

उसे तो बेईमानी के सामने हारना है,

और भले बेईमानी मौज करती रहे,

हमें तो बस इन दुखड़ों के साथ वक़्त गुजरना है।

इस ईमान की वजह से जीना हराम हो गयाहै।

ये मन आज शांत नहीं बैठ रहा,

क्या करूँ परेशान हो गया है।

मगर...... मगर कहीं ना कहीं

उम्मीद जागती है हर रात को,

कोई तो आएगा, जो समझेगा इन जज्बात को,

कंधे भले झुके हुए मगर अभी भी जान है,

आखिर हर पल जो इम्तिहान हो गया है।

ये मन आज शांत नहीं बैठ रहा,

क्या करूँ परेशान हो गया है।

वक़्त का एक सितम है, वो ख़तम हो जाता है,

कलम का लिखा हर शब्द नज़्म हो जाता है।

ख़ामोश हूँ मगर अभी ये ख़ामोशी

मेरी आवाज बन गई है।

अब वो मेरी पहचान हो गया है,

ये शांत बैठ जाएगा बाद थोड़ा सा परेशान हो गया है।

-Hrishikesh Solanki 'Azad"
ID: hrishisolanki31@gmail.com

मज़ा आ गया

ए मोहब्बत तुझे आज़मा के बड़ा मज़ा आया ह,
दिल तो टूटा कई बार, पर मज़ा आया है।

जब सामने वो थी तो बोल न पाते थे कुछ हम,
कई बार अरमानो को दबाया है, पर मज़ा आया है।

कई बार शमा ने मुझसे कहा मत आ मेरे पास,
कई बार खुद को परवाना बनाया है, पर मज़ा आया है।

कई बार कोई राज़ की बात बताते हुए
वो इतने क़रीब आती थी,
उन्हें अक्सर मैंने जज़्बातों को काबू किया है,
पर मज़ा आया है।

अलग हुए थे जब साथ मिलके कभी हम,

इश्क़ को ना मुकम्म्मल छोड़ा है, पर मज़ा आया है।

कई बार अपनी आँखें

ज़माने से छुपाने की कोशिश की है,

कई बार महफ़िलो में खुद को रुस्वा किया है,

पर मज़ा आया है।

-Kazi Imranul Haque
ID: kaziimranul@gmail.com

कभी

कभी अल्फ़ाज़ों को छोड़कर,

आँखों को पढ़ना सीख लेना,

शायद कोई राज़ पता चल जाए!

कभी तारों को छोड़कर

खुले आसमान को देख लीजिएगा,

शायद कोई हमसफ़र याद आ जाए!

कभी मंज़िल को छोड़कर सफर पर गौर फरमाइयेगा,

शायद कोई मुसाफिर ही दिख जाए!

कभी किताबो में मसरूफ होने की जगह खिड़की के

बहार बच्चों को देख लीजिएगा,

शायद दिल में छुपा बच्चा मिलजाए!

कभी तस्वीरो को कैमरा में कैद करने की जगह दिल

और आँखों में कैद कर लीजिएगा,

क्या पता कभी कोई अपना ही याद आजाए!

कभी वृक्ष पर उगने वाले फल और फूल को छोड़कर

पत्तों को भी सहला कर देखिएगा

शायद हरियाली फैल जाए!

कभी पक्षियों को कंकड़ मार कर उड़ने की जगह उन्हें

गगन में उड़ते हुआ देखिएगा

शायद आपका दिल भी ज़ंजीरें तोड़कर आज़ादी

मांगले!

कभी शिकायतों की जगह

खुदा से कोई मन्नत मांगलेना,

क्या पता कोई ख़्वाईश पूरी हो जाए!

-Aastha Mayur Shah
ID: aasthashah2304@yahoo.com

मिट्टी

मिट्टी के बने हम भी।

मिट्टी के बने तुम भी।।

मिट जाना एक दिन हमको भी है।

मिट जाना एक दिन तुमको भी।।

या चिता बनकर जल जाओगे।

या क़फन बनकर गढ़ जाओगे।।

मिट्टी में तुम ऐसे भी मिल जाओगे।

मिट्टी में तुम वैसे भी मिल जाओगे।।

मिट्टी न बोले, "मैं हिन्दु की मिट्टी।"

मिट्टी न बोले, "मैं ईसाई की मिट्टी।"

मिट्टी न बोले, "मैं मुसलमान की मिट्टी।"

मिट्टी तो बोले, "मैं हर इन्सान की मिट्टी।"

जब मिट्टी ने न किया कोई भेद-भाव,

तो मिट्टी के पुतलों में क्यों यह कुःभाव?

क्यों मचाते हम देश के नाम पर आतंक?

क्यों करते हम धर्म की आढ़ में घाव?

क्यों हुए आखिर इस मिट्टी के बँटवारे?

क्यों छूटे इतिहास के पन्नों पे रक्त के फव्वारे?

क्यों बिके मानव व मानवता; कपट के हुए वारे-न्यारे?

सम्बन्धों व नक्शों में दरारें पेश कर,

क्या मिला तुम्हे प्यारे?

पुष्प खिलते हिन्दुस्तान की मिट्टी पर भी।

पुष्प खिलते पाक़िस्तान की मिट्टी पर भी।।

सूरज उगे इस शम्शान की मिट्टी पर भी।

सूर्योदय तो उस क़ब्रिस्तान की मिट्टी पर भी।।

मिट्टी से मिला अस्तित्व हमारा।

मिट्टी में ही है मिलजाना दोबारा।।

मिट्टी से ऊँचा उठने का गुरूर न कर।

स्वयं को मिट्टी से, मिट्टी को स्वयं से दूर न कर।।

मिट्टी के बने हम भी हैं।

मिट्टी के बने तुम भी हो।

मिट जाना एक दिन हमको भी है।

मिट जाना एक दिन तुमको भी है।।

-Rohan Ram Vaswani
ID: rv22894@gmail.com

हिम्मत को तू, ना हार से दबोच

आगे बढ़ता पहला कदम,

हमेशा ही लड़खड़ायेगा।

जीतने की तू आस रख,

नाकोई तुझे रोक पायेगा।

कहानी आज सुनाओ मैं,

वो मासूम सी एक लड़की की।

जो मिसाल है बेहतरीन आज,

इस देश के हर एक व्यक्ति की।

वह शिकारियों में औज़ार लिया,

इज़्ज़त से उसकी खेल लिया।

शकल पर फेरा तेहज़ाब था,

ईश्वर का बिना सोचे अजीब हिसाब था।

जीवन भर का रोना था,

बचने सी बदतर सोना था।

उसकी इन्साफ की आवाज़ दबाई गयी,

डर के ऊपर लड़ाई हुई।

पुलिस ने उससे ना बढ़ने दिया,

यहाँ हार हुई, उससे ना लड़ने दिया।

पर रुकजा उसकी ना रग में था,

परिवार जो हमेशा संग में था।

वह दाती रही बस आगे बढ़ी,

हार की मारी आवाज़ थी छड़ी।

इंसाफ़ की जंग में अब देश भी था,

उसकी हार जो हिम्मत अब था।

आज इन्साफ लिए वह ज़िंदा है,

उन्दरिंदो का शव अब मुर्दा है।

सीख की वह मिसाल बनी,

हिम्मत ने मात, हार की दी।

समझे तुम मेरे प्यारे दोस्त,

हिम्मत को तू, ना हार से दबोच।

-Vrushika Rajesh Vadhavana
ID: vrushika0402@gmail.com

काश

काश वह फिर से हमारी ज़िन्दजी मे आए,

काश वह फिर अपना प्यार मुझपर बरसाए,

काश वह पल वापस आए जब

ऊन का हाथ पकड़के घूमने जाए,

काश वह फिर लौटकर आए और संग मुस्कुराए,

काश आज वह हमारे साथ होते,

काश वह वापस आकर फिर से बोले

"मेरी लाड़ली को कोई कुछ बोलेगा नहीं।"

काश वह आज यहाँ होते,

काश यह ख़्वाब हकीकत मे बदलजाए,

काश वह वापस आजाए।

पर यह काश, काश ही रह जाएगा।

क्यूँकि आज उनके यादों के अलावा

कुछ और नहीं हमारे पास।

क्यूँकि आज उनके यादों के अलावा

कुछ और नहीं हमारे पास।

"दादा जी की लाड़ली"

-Khushboo Kapoor
ID: khushbookapoor2000@gmail.com

माँ

तेरे आँचल की महक दुनिया सँवार देती है,

लबों पे तेरे मेरी दुआ, हर काम बना देती है।

इस ज़ालिम दुनिया में एक तु ही राह दिखाती है,

गलत और सही का अंतर पहचानना सिखाती है।

तेरी अनेक छटाऐं देख मन में आदर आता है,

माँ तेरा काली का रुप भी सरस्वती सा नजर आता है।

अपने आँसू जो तूने मेरे जनम पर बहाए थे,

कसम है उस उपर वाले की

उन मोतीयों को सिफ खुशी के आँसू बनाऐंगे।

मेरी हर खुशी के लिए तुने अपनी चाह त्याग दी,

इस जनम क्या हर जनम तुझे ही अपनी जननी

चाहूँगी।

-Dnyanasi Rahurikar
ID: dnyanasirahurikar@yahoo.com

तूझसे ना रोकना है!!

शुद्ध चरित्र और क्षमता,
खुदकी खुदको ही बनानी है!
तूझे ना रुकना है, तूझसे ना रोकना है!

तोडदे जंजीरे सारी पंख की, मिट्टी पर है तू,
लेकिन भर उडान ऑसमाें की!
तू रक होंसला, मुसीबतों से घबरामत!
अपनी विराटता से, दुनिया को अपनाना है!
तूझे ना रुकना है, तूझसे ना रोकना है!

कोई कहे तो कहे, सरफिरा, पागल तुझे!
अक्सर इतिहास वही लिखते हैं,
जो सरफीरे, पागल कहलाते हैं!

यहाँ, सबेरे से पहले, अंधेरा बहुत गहरा होगा!

दृढ विश्वास है, उजाला अंधेरे से बडा होगा!

बस एक बात यारा,

तूझे ना रुकना है, तूझसे ना रोकना है!

-Rtr. Rahul Shivaji Mohite
ID: drrrahul3170@gmail.com

"भारत"

भगवा, सफ़ेद और हरे से बना है,

ये देश किसी एक रंग की कहानी थोड़ी है।

हिन्दू हो या मुसलमां

किसी एक की मेहरबानी थोड़ी है।

जागीर है पूर्वजों की अगर तो बराबर बँटेंगीं,

नामंजूर है अगर तो आओ मिलकर बोते हैं वो फसल

जो अगली बरसात कटेगी।

आओ हटा कर तीनों रंग एक नई कहानी लिखते हैं।

आओ ज़रा इतिहास नूरानी लिखते हैं।

झंडा फहराते हैं शान से हवा में,

मगर रंग इस बार इंसानी लिखते हैं।

-Rishi Shukla
ID: rishishukla14@gmail.com

कम्बख्त कलम

सरहदी लकीरें पार कर,

ये चट्टानों से जा लड़ती है।

हर जंग की नीतिकार है,

यह विजय मंत्र गड़ती है।

है देखो रामायण इससे,

इससे ही है गीता।

इसके दम पर मन मौजी मतवाला

मजनू अनंत सा लहै जीता।

रच डाली है बाइबल इसने,

कुरान इसी से आई ना होती

तो कोन जानता, राम, रहीम, ईसाई।

जो कुछ तुम को ज्ञात हुआ,

है सब कुछ इसी सेआया।

इसने ही तो देखो बच्चू देखो समय को काल बताया।

तेज़ है इसकी धार, स्याही सदाही गहरी

कहां किसी के कह देने से यह ज़रा भी ठहरी।

देखो कितनी निडर,

सियासत से ना डरती है।

कह कर अपनी बात ही कागज पर, दम भर्ती है।

ना कोई खुदा है इसका,

ना ही कोई धरम है।

सदैव सत्य शिला लेख लिखती,

यह कमबख्त कलम है।

-Rishi Shukla
ID: rishishukla14@gmail.com

सुदामा बने कन्हैया

कैसी मायानगरी भैया सोया है

सिपहै या पैसा दिन दिन छोटा है

पर सबसे बड़ा रुपैया।

अदालत किं साब फाइल खा गई,

अंदर बैठी चुहिया जनका धन भी गायब,

देखो सुदामा बने कन्हैया

हमारा भी सबका गज़ खा गई,

मैया मोरी गैया कहा से तुमको अब दिखलाएं,

बोलो मोटा भैया

प्यार की थोड़ी बात करो

तो कहते है हाय दैया बिरयानी खाने गए थे घरतक,

अपने जगत घुमैया

सारा सच है इनका,

माने सर्कट और मुन्ना भैया

झूठ की ट्रेन पर खड़े हैं

करते दोनों छैयां छैयां।

-Rishi Shukla
ID: rishishukla14@gmail.com

पा लिया सब कुछ

कुछ पाने की कोशिश मैं मैंने,
खुद को ही खो दिया।
दिखावे की शानो शौकत मैं,
अपनों को पीछे छोड़ दिया।

पा तो लिया वह सब कुछ मैंने,
जो औरो मैं मुझे भाता था।
पा लिया वह नाम जिससे मुझे
कोई और पुकारना चाहता था।

वह मुकाम भी पालिया मैंने,
जो किसी वक़्त ऊँचा दिखता था।
पार करली वह सिडियाँ भी,
जहाँ से बार बार मैं गिरता था।

लेकिन कुछ पाने की कोशिश में मैंने,

खुदको ही खो दिया।

जीतने के बाद भी मेरा दिल,

नाजाने क्यों रो दिया।

-Yash Agrawal
ID: yashb4u.agrawal@gmail.com

क्यों ए दिल

बंद हैं आँखें,

पर उन्ही पे नज़र है।

ख़यालों में सिर्फ

उन काही ज़िक्र है।

क्यों ए दिल

तू करता फ़िक्र है।

यह तो महज़

उनके हुस्न का असर है।

-ReyHan
ID: sshreyang@gmail.com

गुरूर-ही-माँ

अब बचपन इतना सुहाना क्यों लगता है ,

जब बड़े होने की ख्वाहिश थी ही

उस उम्र से शायद पकड़ लिया था

माँ ने हाथ शिद्दत से इतनी,

के अब किस्मत भी पूछे की कहाँ गयी वो लकीरे

चलते थे हम जिसके दम पे ...

मुश्किलें भी बोहोत आयी है,

और उससे बड़ा खुदको समझने वाले लोग भी

पर आँखों मे नमी तो इस बात छायी है

की इनसे भिड़ने की तालीम सीखने वाले को

ही भुला देने से बड़ा ना होगा कोई अफ़सोस भी ...

आ जाती है अपनी बातो से दूर करने अधूरेपन को ये

दुनिया बीच बीच मे हज़ारो बार ,

अब इन मतलबी बेगानो को कौन समझाए ,

की ख़ामोशी से पूरा कर देती है

मुझे वो खिला कर उसके हाथो

का खाना बस एक ही बार

खूबियों से अपनी वाक़िफ़ हो कर भी ,

मंज़ूरी तलाशा करते है गैरो की

पर यारा पूछा नहीं कभी माँ से अपनी ,

की क्यों तराशा करती है वो मेरी खामियों को भी

घर का मतलब होता क्या है ,

ये पूछो ना ज़रा हम जज़्बाती मुसाफिरों से

ईंट के सजे और माँ के सहेजे मे फर्क ना समझा दिया ,

तो बंद करदेंगे देना भगवन का दर्जा आज से

उसे अब शर्म नहीं है कोई

ज़िन्दगी भर तेरे पल्लू से बांधने मे,

एक तू ही तो मिशाल अमर है

मेरी उसकी भी उम्र ढल जाये,

तो घूम जाएंगे कही

इस अँधेरी दुनिया के साथ एक होने मे

ऐसा क्या है आखिर एक आम औरत मे ,

जो लिख डालते है पैन तारीफ मे उसकी

अब इसमें हमारा क्या कसूर है जनाब ,

जब लिख डाला हो इतिहास

खुद उसने झांसी थी जिसकी

-Sanya Dutta
ID: sanyadutta16@gmail.com

आज़ादी

आज़ादी उड़ते पंख भी कट जायेंगे ,

ऐसी आज़ादी है,

कुछ बूँदें बची हैं पीने की,

पानी की और लहू की,

ऐसी तबाही की निशानी है,

भूखा मरा है कोई राह पर,

और कुछ लालच में,

माँ भी रोई है, और बेटी भी,

किसी ने छोड़ी जो एक बड़ी निशानी है,

कुछ बेटे तोः सरहद पे सर क़ुर्बान कर आये,

कुछ नशे में कटवा कर आये हैं!

मानलो ये झूठी आज़ादी तुम,

तुम्हारे ढोंग की यह निशानी है !

-Rajat Prabhakar
ID: rajatprabhakar94@gmail.com

कश्मकश

कश्मकश सी है, पर क्यों?

समझ आ जाये अगर,

तो मज़ा क्या है सोचा था,

लिखने बैठूँगी जब तो कहानी लिखूँगी पर,

सोचके लिखने में रखा क्या है।

क्या, क्यों, कब और कैसे?

नहीं करोगे फिर सवाल ऐसे,

जब जानोगे राज़ की हमें ज़िन्दगी में पता क्या है

ख़ुद को सुनो, उसी को समझो,

समझ जाओ तो देखो,

इस दुनिया से लापता क्या है।

इन्सान से धोखा, इन्सान को दबाना,

है काम इन्सान का,

इंसानियत के नाम पे अब बचा क्या है।

जितना समझा, लिखदिया अब

तुम अधूरी कहो या पूरी,

बताओ, इसमें मेरी ख़ता क्या है?

-Bhupinder Kaur
ID: bhupinderghuman27@gmail.com

मैं कैसे आपको रोकू भला?

मै कैसे चुप बैठूँ? वो हम उम्र मेरे, वो साथी मेरे,

लटपट हो रहे लहू से।

जो सोचना सकूँ मे सपने में भी,

गुज़र रहे वो ऐसी गर्दिशों से।

हर हाथ में जो लहरा रहा तिरंगा

पुकारे मुझे तो मै कैसे घर बैठूँ भला?

चिल्ला रहा जब जो शहर भारतवासी में,

तो मैं कैसे चुप बैठूँ भला?

जात – पात, रीत- रिवाज़ की फ़िक्र भूल के उतर गया,

जब उतर गया हर उम्र का भारतवासी सड़क पे

मैं कैसे बेफिक्र घूमूँ भला?

भूख प्यास भूल के बस

कर के याद वो नाइंसाफी, वो बेरहमी,

दिल में ज़स्बा और लबों पे बस एक ही नारा,

"अरे छीन के लेंगे आज़ादी"

लेके जब हो रही अपने हक़ के लिए लड़ाई

मै कैसे चैन से रोटी खाऊँ भला?

जो सिगरतट के छले साथ बनाते थे यार

आज खड़े है बनके एक ही आवाज़

जो अंजान हैं दुःख सुख दीन दुनिया से,

वो नन्हे हाथ भी दे रहे हैं साथ।

खौल रहा खून उनका भी

जो बिता चुके अपनी जवानी के साल।

ख़ामोशी को कमज़ोरी समझने लगे है जो,

उनके आगे मै कैसे सर झुकाऊँ भला?

तो कैसे के जुटे, जेब में भर के खूब सारा हौसला

निकल पड़ी मै भी अपना फ़र्ज़ निभाने।

कुछ देखे और लाखो अनदेखे चेहरे,

बोल रहे थे वो इंक़लाब ज़िंदाबाद

और आँखों में था आक्रोश बेहिसाब।

मिलके हमने लड़ी एक बार फिर आज़ादी की लड़ाई,

रुकेंगे नहीं जब तक हो नहीं जाती सुनवाई।

कलम बोले या बोले आपके अलफ़ाज़,

आवाज़ उठाए बिना

नाइंसाफ़ी के खिलाफ लेना तुम ना सांस।

जब हिंदुस्तान बोल रहा है आवाज़ उठाओ आप,

मै कैसे आपको रोकूँ भला?

- Anjali Kochhar
ID: anjalikochhar29@gmail.com

गालियाँ

यह रास्ते, यह गांव की गलियां,

बितायी है यहाँ जैसे साड़ियां...

कई खूबसूरत रिश्ते है बनाये,

कई अनगिनत सपने है सजाये...

वोः वक़्त भी क्या वक़्त था,

जब लोगो के पास एक दूजे के लिए वक़्त था...

चाहे हो किसीके भी खुशियों

और गम पे सबका बराबर हक़ था....

हर मौसम का मज़ा लेते थे....

तीज त्यौहार के रंग यूँ खिलते थे...

कुछ अनोखी हुआ करती थी वोः दिवाली,

जो सब मिलके मनाया करते थे....

अच्छे हो दिन चाहे बुरे,

चाहे कितनी ही काली क्यों न होती रात....

आसान हो जाती चाहे जैसी भी हो कठिनाई,

बात जो लिया करते थे जसबाट....

वोः दौर ही कुछ अलग, कुछ अद्भुत था,

दोस्त महफ़िल और परिवार का था संग..

खिल खिलते हुए बीते यहाँ ज़िन्दगी,

थी एक अलग ही उमंग, एक अलग ही तरंग....

आज जब जाने का वक़्त है आया,

न जाने क्यों यह मन भर आया ....

जा रहे है जिस नयी गली की और,

ऊँची इमारते, बंद दरवाज़े...

क्या कोई यहाँ अपना कहलाने लायक बन पायेगा,

या यह दिल अपनों की तलाश में

अकेला रह जाएगा???

-Bhakti Bhuta
Email ID: bhaktibhuta91@gmail.com

चाय

हाँ मैं एक चाय हूँ।
क्या आप को चाय से बेहद प्यार है?
चलो आपको चाय के बारे मे
कुछ देखी सुनी बाते बताता हूँ।।

रिश्तों का मेल जोल भी कितना अजी बहोता है,
दो अजनबी रिश्तों को मिलाने वाला भी
एक "चाय" होता है।

भीड़ भरी दुनिया में कोई जिंदगी भर साथ देता है,
या कोई यूँ बीच डगर में ही साथ छोड़ देता है।

फिर एक शाम चाय अपनी जगह लेता है,
और एक चुस्की चाय सारे गम भुला देता है।।

मैं एक चाय हूँ,
जुल्मत में भी मुस्कराऊंगा,
ए इंसान मुझे संभाल कर रखना,
मैं वक्त पर हमेशा काम आऊंगा।

अरे!! पर चाय का साथ कहाँ तक है?

तो सुनो...

दो दिल मिल रहे है,
पर चाय साथ में है।

पैसो का लेन देन हो रहा है,
चाय का साथ उस वक्त भी होता है।

नेता और राजनेता चुप छुपाकर घोटाले कर रहे है,
चाय उस समय भी होता है।

पढाई करते करते नींद आजाए,
तो भी चाय साथ ही है।

रेलगाड़ी का लंबा समय काट रहे हो,

बस चाय का ही साथ है।

बेरोजगारी की चिंता है,
पर चाय आपके साथ है।

कामयाबी नहीं मिल रही,
फिर भी चाय आपके साथ है।

दोस्त, दुनिया या परिवार ने आपका साथ छोड़ दिया,
पर अब भी चाय आपके साथ है।

प्रेमिका ने आपका साथ छोड़ दिया,
अरे ये क्या आज भी चाय आप के साथ ही है।

याद रखना....

जिंदगी में पत्नी सात जन्मों का साथ दे या न दे,
पर एक चाय आपका सात जन्मो तक देगी,
और...

बेरोजगारी और नाकामयाबी के वक्त
दुनिया बहुत ताने मारेगी,

इन सब तानो से थककर आपकी थकान मिटाने के
लिए "चाय" ही अपना जग हलेगी।
ये सब सुनते सुनते "चाय" बी बोलपड़ा,
"मालूम है कोई मोल नहीं मेरा, फिर भी
कुछ अनमोल लोगो से रिश्ता रखता हूँ।"

एक इंसान भले ही एक इंसान को ना परख पाए,
मैं हर तरह के इंसान को परख ता हूँ।

एक इंसान ही इंसान को
दुनिया भर के तकलीफ देता है,
पर मेरी एक चुस्की जब इंसान लेता है,
पल भर के लिए ही सही
पर सारी तकलीफ़ें मिटा देता है।

हाँ मैं एक चाय हूँ,

पर सच में खुश हूँ और सबको खुश रखता हूँ,

थोड़ा सा गर्म और लापरवाह हूँ

फिर भी सबकी परवाह करता हूँ।।

हाँ मैं एक चाय हूँ।

- Ashutosh Dubey
ID: advashutoshjdubey@gmail.com

चुप हो गया

जो होना था वो हो गया,

धुएं की तरह खो गया।

हर बार यही सोच रख,

खुद को संभालता गया।

ये कैसी वेदना है की चुप हो गया।

क्यों आत्मा तेरी चीत्कार रही,

हुँकार रही, दर्शा रही की देख,

की देख, स्वयं का चित्र।

ये नीरस दृश रक्त ही है,

जो बहर हा, कुछ कह रहा।

मैं धैर्य का प्रमाणन ही,

प्रतीक या तना का हूँ।

जो चेतना पेढ हर हा,

सब मौन हो कर सह रहा,

फिर क्यों गरजता नही,

क्यों रोकता उस रक्त को

जो चक्षुयो से बह रहा।

ये व्यथा है वक्तव्य प्रार्थी,
आ तेरी आत्मा का अंश है।
क्यों मुह मोड़कर चल रहा,
सूर्य क्यों तेरे आंगन में ढल रहा?
कब अन्धेरे में खो गया,
ये कैसी वेदना है की चुप हो गया।

व्यभिचारीता का पड़ाव है,
एक मानसिक सड़ाव है।
खुदका आंकलन तो कर,
स्वयं का संकलन तो कर।
ये चेतना का तिरस्कार है
या अंधकार का अविष्कार है,
ये द्वंद कबतक खेलेगा,
तू सोचता है सब अकेले झेलेगा?

वो ऐसा था, सब वैसा था

तू कैसा था, ये किसका था।

ये होने का ही तो भ्रम है पगले,

की कुछ "होना" वर्तमान का प्रतीक है।

एक दीप है, एक गीत है, उम्मीद है, पर ठीक है,

तू वर्तमान का साक्षन ही,

तू भूत का प्रमान है।

अब "होने" को कुछ बचा नही,

सब "था" में बदल गया।

ये कैसी वेदना है की चुप हो गया।

- Shubham Jha
ID: shubham.jha22@gmail.com

माँ

जब से मैं इस दुनिया में आया हूँ,

जबसे मैं उसकी गोद में समाया हूँ,

तबसे मेरी मुस्कराहट ही उसका जूनून है।

मुझे तकलीफों से दूर रखना ही उसका सुकून है।

रातों को उसका जागना ताकि मैं चैन से सो सकूँ।

मेरी हर ज़िद्द को पूरा कर नाता कि मैं खुश हो सकूँ।

चोट मुझे लगती थी तो दर्द उसे भी होता था।

आँखें उसकी भी नम होती जब जब मैं रोता था।

सारे कष्ट तुझसे दूर हो ये मन्नत है मेरी।

तेरे साथ गुज़रता हर वो लम्हा जन्नत है मेरी।

खुशनसीब हूँ, तू मेरे साथ है आज भी माँ,

तेरी दुआओं ने ही सलामत रखा है आज भी माँ।

शायद मैं कभी कहना पाया लेकिन,

बेहद्द प्यार करता हूँ तुझसे आज भी माँ।

-Hrithik Rohora
ID: hrithikrohora@gmail.com

कहानी बदल नहीं सकता,
तो सोचता क्यों है

जब कोई हल ही नहीं तो फिर खोजता क्यों है ?
हाँ जो तू चाहता था वो हो नहीं सकता,
पर ज़िन्दगी भर ऐसे तू रो नहीं सकता।
माना तेरी ज़िन्दगी का सबसे बुरा वक्त है,
लेकिन इस वजह से तू सबकुछ खो नहीं सकता।
जो तेरे हाथ में था वो तूने किया है,
खुशियों के बिना भी तू ज़िन्दगी जिया है।.
शायद पूरी तरह से तो नहीं पर,
ज़ख्म का कुछ हिस्सा तो तूने सीया है।
पहले जैसा था शायद होगा ना फिर कभी,
खुशियों के पहले ही आते है गुम्म सभी।
वक्त को वक्त दे इस बार भी बदलेगा,
मिटा देगा सारे दर्द जो मौजूद है अभी।

-Hrithik Rohora
ID: hrithikrohora@gmail.com

सब संभल जाएगा

ये पल ये वक़्त यू निकल जाएगा,

देखते ही देखते सब संभल जाएगा।

डर की ये रात जल्द ही कट जाएगी,

हौसला ना हारो उम्मीद भरी सुबह जल्द ही जाएगी।

सोचा मैंने क्या रह सा गया,

दिल की सारी बात कह ता गया।

नहीं मिलता आसानी से ऐसा मौका,

करलो आराम से ज़िन्दगी का लेखा जोखा।

ना करो इन् विपरीत स्तिथि को बदनाम,

सयम और संकल्प लाएगा समाधान।

ये पल ये वक़्त यू निकल जाएगा,

देखते ही देखते सब संभल जाएगा।

-Pratik Shah
Email ID: pratik.82621@gmail.com

आखिर आ ही गया
ज़िन्दगी मैं वो पल।

आखिर आ ही गया ज़िन्दगी मैं वो पल

उनके दर्द भरे ज़ख्म भी कहलाये गए गुज़रा हुआ कल।

छोड़ आये प्यार की वह गलियाँ,

जहा धुंदली से हो गयी थी दुनिया।

आदतों ने कर दिए था उन्हें

जीने के लिए इस कदर मजबूर,

अगर ज़िंदा थे वो तो सिर्फ उसी की लिए हुज़ूर।

कमज़ोर दिल पर हुआ ऐसा दर्द भरा सितम,

की हर पल लगे मानो

शराब के बिना तो निकल ही जायेगा दम।

हसी की बीच आंसू दबाए हर एक पल वो रोया,

क्युकी सच्चा प्यार ना था उनके नसीब में बोया।

फिर जगी एक उम्मीद की किरण,

ज़िन्दगी मैं छाया खुशियों का वशीकरण।

गिरकर सँभालने लगे थे वो,

उठकर फिर चलने लगे थे वो।

मंज़िल को हासिल करने का जूनून,

उन्हें पोहचने लगा था सुकून।

कामियाबी की वो ऊंचाई,

मापने ना देती उन्हें अपने दिल की गहराई।

लेकिन वक़्त के पन्नो में छुपे थे कुछ ऐसे सवाल,

जिनके जवाबो का इंतज़ार

आज भी मचा रहा है उनके दिल में बवाल।

-Harshita Sewani
ID: rtr.harshita.sewani@gmail.com

ख़ामोशी

पता नहीं क्या हुआ था ,चुप सी रेहनी लगी थी मैं मानो

अपने से ही सीमित हो गयी थी।

अक्सर भूल जाती चीज़ो को,

बस खो जाती आस पास के नज़रो मैं।

चेहरा कहना चाहता है कुछ,

मैं कहना चाहती हूँ बहुत कुछ;

और वो साड़ी आवाज़ें अंदर गूंज रही है,

बेहोश कर रही है - मदहोश कर रही है,

बस अब दर्द कर रही है।

अब खामोश हूँ और वजह नहीं है

क्यूँकि कहने के लिए लोग नहीं है,

शब्द नहीं है और

वजूद नहीं है मेरी बातो का मेरे शब्दों का;

बस अब खामोश ही रहना चाहती हूँ।

- Arti Chheda
ID: artichheda01@gmail.com

Who Are We?

Dreams are limitless and so is our vision. Being **India's 1st "Lead by Authors" Publication House**, Lapsus Creations connect your dreams with vision.

With our Guided Publishing approach, authors will have their own dedicated team of experts working alongside for their **BOOK** to come alive. We guide them from the very initial stage of their writing journey till, and after the book is successfully published. While keeping quality at the forefront, we understand the needs of a writer and work towards fulfilling them at zero extra cost.

Promoting creativity across the world is what we are determined about. While we work on the dreams of our authors, we alongside take care of their choices too.

With Lapsus Creations authors have the leverage to choose what they want for their dream book. We firmly believe in, **Of the Authors, By the Authors, For the Authors.**

Every dream has the right to get connected to its vision and Lapsus Creations has taken this initiative. Publishing every dream is our vision and hence we thrive on our motto **DREAM! VISION! LET'S CONNECT?**